W0254627

The Man of Destiny

by Bernard Shaw

The twelfth of May, 1796, in north Italy, at Tavazzano, on the road from Lodi to Milan. The afternoon sun is blazing serenely over the plains of Lombardy, treating the Alps with respect and the anthills with indulgence, not incommoded by the basking of the swine and oxen in the villages nor hurt by its cool reception in the churches, but fiercely disdainful of two hordes of mischievous insects which are the French and Austrian armies. Two days before, at Lodi, the Austrians tried to prevent the French from crossing the river by the narrow bridge there; but the French, commanded by a general aged 27, Napoleon Bonaparte, who does not understand the art of war, rushed the fireswept bridge, supported by a tremendous cannonade in which the young general assisted with his own hands. Cannonading is his technical specialty; he has been trained in the artillery under the old regime, and made perfect in the military arts of shirking his duties, swindling the paymaster over travelling expenses, and dignifying war with the noise and smoke of cannon, as depicted in all military portraits. He is, however, an original observer, and has perceived, for the first time since the invention of gunpowder, that a cannon ball, if it strikes a man, will kill him. To a thorough grasp of this remarkable discovery, he adds a highly evolved faculty for physical geography and for the calculation of times and distances. He has prodigious powers of work, and a clear, realistic knowledge of human nature in public affairs, having seen it exhaustively tested in that department during the French Revolution. He is imaginative without illusions, and creative without religion, loyalty, patriotism or any of the common ideals. Not that he is incapable of these ideals: on the contrary, he has swallowed them all in his boyhood, and now, having a keen dramatic faculty, is extremely clever at playing upon them by the arts of the actor and stage manager. Withal, he is no spoiled child. Poverty, ill-luck, the shifts of impecunious shabby-gentility, repeated failure as a would-be author, humiliation as a rebuffed time server, reproof and punishment as an incompetent and dishonest officer, an escape from dismissal from the service so narrow that if the emigration of the nobles had not raised the value of even the most rascally lieutenant to the famine price of a general he would have been swept contemptuously from the army: these trials have ground the conceit out of him, and forced him to be self-sufficient and to understand that to such men as he is the world will give nothing that he cannot take from it by force. In this the world is not free from cowardice and folly; for Napoleon, as a merciless cannonader of political rubbish, is making himself useful. indeed, it is even now impossible to live in England without sometimes feeling how much that country lost in not being conquered by him as well as by Julius Caesar.

However, on this May afternoon in 1796, it is early days with him. He is only 26, and has but recently become a general, partly by using his wife to seduce the Directory (then governing France) partly by the scarcity of officers caused by the emigration as aforesaid; partly by his faculty of knowing a country, with all its roads, rivers, hills and valleys, as he knows the palm of his hand; and largely by that new faith of his in the efficacy of firing cannons at people. His army is, as to discipline, in a state which has so greatly shocked some modern writers before whom the following story has been enacted, that they, impressed with the later glory of "L'Empereur," have altogether refused to credit it. But Napoleon is not "L'Empereur" yet: he has only just been dubbed "Le Petit Caporal," and is in the stage of gaining influence over his men by displays of pluck. He is not in a position to force his will on them, in orthodox military fashion, by the cat o' nine tails. The French Revolution, which has escaped suppression solely through the monarchy's habit of being at least four years in arrear with its soldiers in the matter of pay, has substituted for that habit, as far as possible, the habit of not paying at all, except in promises and patriotic flatteries which are not compatible with martial law of the Prussian type. Napoleon has therefore approached the Alps in command of men without money, in rags, and consequently indisposed to stand much discipline, especially from upstart generals. This circumstance, which would have embarrassed an idealist soldier, has been worth a thousand cannon to Napoleon. He has said to his army, "You have patriotism and courage; but you have no money, no clothes, and deplorably indifferent food. In Italy there are all these things, and glory as well, to be gained by a devoted army led by a general who regards loot as the natural right of the soldier. I am such a general. En avant, mes enfants!" The result has entirely justified him. The army conquers Italy as the locusts conquered Cyprus. They fight all day and march all night, covering impossible distances and appearing in incredible places, not because every soldier carries a field marshal's baton in his knapsack, but because he hopes to carry at least half a dozen silver forks there next day.

It must be understood, by the way, that the French army does not make war on the Italians. It is there to rescue them from the tyranny of their Austrian conquerors, and confer republican institutions on them; so that in incidentally looting them, it merely makes free with the property of its friends, who ought to be grateful to it, and perhaps would be if ingratitude were not the proverbial failing of their country. The Austrians, whom it fights, are a thoroughly respectable regular army, well disciplined, commanded by gentlemen trained and versed in the art of war: at the head of them Beaulieu, practising the classic art of war under orders from Vienna, and getting horribly beaten by Napoleon, who acts on his own responsibility in defiance of professional precedents or orders from Paris. Even when the Austrians win a battle, all that is necessary is to wait until their routine obliges them to return to their quarters for afternoon tea, so to speak, and win it back again from them: a course pursued later on with brilliant success at Marengo. On the whole, with his foe handicapped by Austrian statesmanship, classic generalship, and the exigencies of the aristocratic social structure of Viennese society, Napoleon finds it possible to be irresistible without working heroic miracles. The world, however, likes miracles and heroes, and is quite incapable of conceiving the action of such forces as academic militarism or Viennese drawing-roomism. Hence it has already begun to manufacture "L'Empereur," and thus to make it difficult for the romanticists of a hundred years later to credit the little scene now in question at Tavazzano as aforesaid.

The best quarters at Tavazzano are at a little inn, the first house reached by travellers passing through the place from Milan to Lodi. It stands in a vineyard; and its principal room, a pleasant refuge from the summer heat, is open so widely at the back to this vineyard that it is almost a large veranda. The bolder children, much excited by the alarums and excursions of the past few days, and by an irruption of French troops at six o'clock, know that the

French commander has quartered himself in this room, and are divided between a craving to peep in at the front windows and a mortal terror of the sentinel, a young gentleman-soldier, who, having no natural moustache, has had a most ferocious one painted on his face with boot blacking by his sergeant. As his heavy uniform, like all the uniforms of that day, is designed for parade without the least reference to his health or comfort, he perspires profusely in the sun; and his painted moustache has run in little streaks down his chin and round his neck except where it has dried in stiff japanned flakes, and had its sweeping outline chipped off in grotesque little bays and headlands, making him unspeakably ridiculous in the eye of History a hundred years later, but monstrous and horrible to the contemporary north Italian infant, to whom nothing would seem more natural than that he should relieve the monotony of his guard by pitchforking a stray child up on his bayonet, and eating it uncooked. Nevertheless one girl of bad character, in whom an instinct of privilege with soldiers is already dawning, does peep in at the safest window for a moment, before a glance and a clink from the sentinel sends her flying. Most of what she sees she has seen before: the vineyard at the back, with the old winepress and a cart among the vines; the door close down on her right leading to the inn entry; the landlord's best sideboard, now in full action for dinner, further back on the same side; the fireplace on the other side, with a couch near it, and another door, leading to the inner rooms, between it and the vineyard; and the table in the middle with its repast of Milanese risotto, cheese, grapes, bread, olives, and a big wickered flask of red wine.

The landlord, Giuseppe Grandi, is also no novelty. He is a swarthy, vivacious, shrewdly cheerful, black-curled, bullet headed, grinning little man of 40. Naturally an excellent host, he is in quite special spirits this evening at his good fortune in having the French commander as his guest to protect him against the license of the troops, and actually sports a pair of gold earrings which he would otherwise have hidden carefully under the winepress with his little equipment of silver plate.

Napoleon, sitting facing her on the further side of the table, and Napoleon's hat, sword and riding whip lying on the couch, she sees for the first time. He is working hard, partly at his meal, which he has discovered how to dispatch, by attacking all the courses simultaneously, in ten minutes (this practice is the beginning of his downfall), and partly at a map which he is correcting from memory, occasionally marking the position of the forces by taking a grapeskin from his mouth and planting it on the map with his thumb like a wafer. He has a supply of writing materials before him mixed up in disorder with the dishes and cruets; and his long hair gets sometimes into the risotto gravy and sometimes into the ink.

GIUSEPPE. Will your excellency—

NAPOLEON (intent on his map, but cramming himself mechanically with his left hand). Don't talk. I'm busy.

GIUSEPPE (with perfect goodhumor). Excellency: I obey.

NAPOLEON. Some red ink.

GIUSEPPE. Alas! excellency, there is none.

NAPOLEON (with Corsican facetiousness). Kill something and bring me its blood.

GIUSEPPE (grinning). There is nothing but your excellency's horse, the sentinel, the lady upstairs, and my wife.

NAPOLEON. Kill your wife.

GIUSEPPE. Willingly, your excellency; but unhappily I am not strong enough. She would kill me.

NAPOLEON. That will do equally well.

GIUSEPPE. Your excellency does me too much honor. (Stretching his hand toward the flask.) Perhaps some wine will answer your excellency's purpose.

NAPOLEON (hastily protecting the flask, and becoming quite serious). Wine! No: that would be waste. You are all the same: waste! waste! waste! (He marks the map with gravy, using his fork as a pen.) Clear away. (He finishes his wine; pushes back his chair; and uses his napkin, stretching his legs and leaning back, but still frowning and thinking.)

GIUSEPPE (clearing the table and removing the things to a tray on the sideboard). Every man to his trade, excellency. We innkeepers have plenty of cheap wine: we think nothing of spilling it. You great generals have plenty of cheap blood: you think nothing of spilling it. Is it not so, excellency?

NAPOLEON. Blood costs nothing: wine costs money. (He rises and goes to the fireplace.)

GIUSEPPE. They say you are careful of everything except human life, excellency.

NAPOLEON. Human life, my friend, is the only thing that takes care of itself. (He throws himself at his ease on the couch.)

GIUSEPPE (admiring him). Ah, excellency, what fools we all are beside you! If I could only find out the secret of your success!

NAPOLEON. You would make yourself Emperor of Italy, eh?

GIUSEPPE. Too troublesome, excellency: I leave all that to you. Besides, what would become of my inn if I were Emperor? See how you enjoy looking on at me whilst I keep the inn for you and wait on you! Well, I shall enjoy looking on at you whilst you become Emperor of Europe, and govern the country for me. (Whilst he chatters, he takes the cloth off without removing the map and inkstand, and takes the corners in his hands and the middle of the edge in his mouth, to fold it up.)

NAPOLEON. Emperor of Europe, eh? Why only Europe?

GIUSEPPE. Why, indeed? Emperor of the world, excellency! Why not? (He folds and rolls up the cloth, emphasizing his phrases by the steps of the process.) One man is like another (fold): one country is like another (fold): one battle is like another. (At the last fold, he slaps the cloth on the table and deftly rolls it up, adding, by way of peroration) Conquer one: conquer all. (He takes the cloth to the sideboard, and puts it in a drawer.)

NAPOLEON. And govern for all; fight for all; be everybody's servant under cover of being everybody's master: Giuseppe.

GIUSEPPE (at the sideboard). Excellency.

NAPOLEON. I forbid you to talk to me about myself.

GIUSEPPE (coming to the foot of the couch). Pardon. Your excellency is so unlike other great men. It is the subject they like best.

NAPOLEON. Well, talk to me about the subject they like next best, whatever that may be.

GIUSEPPE (unabashed). Willingly, your excellency. Has your excellency by any chance caught a glimpse of the lady upstairs?

(Napoleon promptly sits up and looks at him with an interest which entirely justifies the implied epigram.)

NAPOLEON. How old is she?

GIUSEPPE. The right age, excellency.

NAPOLEON. Do you mean seventeen or thirty?

GIUSEPPE. Thirty, excellency.

NAPOLEON. Goodlooking?

GIUSEPPE. I cannot see with your excellency's eyes: every man must judge that for himself. In my opinion, excellency, a fine figure of a lady. (Slyly.) Shall I lay the table for her collation here?

NAPOLEON (brusquely, rising). No: lay nothing here until the officer for whom I am waiting comes back. (He looks at his watch, and takes to walking to and fro between the fireplace and the vineyard.)

GIUSEPPE (with conviction). Excellency: believe me, he has been captured by the accursed Austrians. He dare not keep you waiting if he were at liberty.

NAPOLEON (turning at the edge of the shadow of the veranda). Giuseppe: if that turns out to be true, it will put me into such a temper that nothing short of hanging you and your whole household, including the lady upstairs, will satisfy me.

GIUSEPPE. We are all cheerfully at your excellency's disposal, except the lady. I cannot answer for her; but no lady could resist you, General.

NAPOLEON (sourly, resuming his march). Hm! You will never be hanged. There is no satisfaction in hanging a man who does not object to it.

GIUSEPPE (sympathetically). Not the least in the world, excellency: is there? (Napoleon again looks at his watch, evidently growing anxious.) Ah, one can see that you are a great man, General: you know how to wait. If it were a corporal now, or a sub-lieutenant, at the end of three minutes he would be swearing, fuming, threatening, pulling the house about our ears.

NAPOLEON. Giuseppe: your flatteries are insufferable. Go and talk outside. (He sits down again at the table, with his jaws in his hands, and his elbows propped on the map, poring over it with a troubled expression.)

GIUSEPPE. Willingly, your excellency. You shall not be disturbed. (He takes up the tray and prepares to withdraw.)

NAPOLEON. The moment he comes back, send him to me.

GIUSEPPE. Instantaneously, your excellency.

A LADY'S VOICE (calling from some distant part of the inn). Giusep-pe! (The voice is very musical, and the two final notes make an ascending interval.)

NAPOLEON (startled). What's that? What's that?

GIUSEPPE (resting the end of his tray on the table and leaning over to speak the more confidentially). The lady, excellency.

NAPOLEON (absently). Yes. What lady? Whose lady?

GIUSEPPE. The strange lady, excellency.

NAPOLEON. What strange lady?

GIUSEPPE (with a shrug). Who knows? She arrived here half an hour before you in a hired carriage belonging to the Golden Eagle at Borghetto. Actually by herself, excellency. No servants. A dressing bag and a trunk: that is all. The postillion says she left a horse—a charger, with military trappings, at the Golden Eagle.

NAPOLEON. A woman with a charger! That's extraordinary.

THE LADY'S VOICE (the two final notes now making a peremptory descending interval). Giuseppe!

NAPOLEON (rising to listen). That's an interesting voice.

GIUSEPPE. She is an interesting lady, excellency. (Calling.) Coming, lady, coming. (He makes for the inner door.)

NAPOLEON (arresting him with a strong hand on his shoulder). Stop. Let her come.

VOICE. Giuseppe!! (Impatiently.)

GIUSEPPE (pleadingly). Let me go, excellency. It is my point of honor as an innkeeper to come when I am called. I appeal to you as a soldier.

A MAN's VOICE (outside, at the inn door, shouting). Here, someone. Hello! Landlord. Where are you? (Somebody raps vigorously with a whip handle on a bench in the passage.)

NAPOLEON (suddenly becoming the commanding officer again and throwing Giuseppe off). There he is at last. (Pointing to the inner door.) Go. Attend to your business: the lady is calling you. (He goes to the fireplace and stands with his back to it with a determined military air.)

GIUSEPPE (with bated breath, snatching up his tray). Certainly, excellency. (He hurries out by the inner door.)

THE MAN's VOICE (impatiently). Are you all asleep here? (The door opposite the fireplace is kicked rudely open; and a dusty sub-lieutenant bursts into the room. He is a chuckle-headed young man of 24, with the fair, delicate, clear skin of a man of rank, and a self-assurance on that ground which the French Revolution has failed to shake in the smallest degree. He has a thick silly lip, an eager credulous eye, an obstinate nose, and a loud confident voice. A young man without fear, without reverence, without imagination, without sense, hopelessly insusceptible to the Napoleonic or any other idea, stupendously egotistical, eminently qualified to rush in where angels fear to tread, yet of a vigorous babbling vitality which bustles him into the thick of things. He is just now boiling with vexation, attributable by a superficial observer to his impatience at not being promptly attended to by the staff of the inn, but in which a more discerning eye can perceive a certain moral depth, indicating a more permanent and momentous grievance. On seeing Napoleon, he is sufficiently taken aback to check himself and salute; but he does not betray by his manner any of that prophetic consciousness of Marengo and Austerlitz, Waterloo and St. Helena, or the Napoleonic pictures of Delaroche and Meissonier, which modern culture will instinctively expect from him.)

NAPOLEON (sharply). Well, sir, here you are at last. Your instructions were that I should arrive here at six, and that I was to find you waiting for me with my mail from Paris and with despatches. It is now twenty minutes to eight. You were sent on this service as a hard rider with the fastest horse in the camp. You arrive a hundred minutes late, on foot. Where is your horse!

THE LIEUTENANT (moodily pulling off his gloves and dashing them with his cap and whip on the table). Ah! where indeed? That's just what I should like to know, General. (With emotion.) You don't know how fond I was of that horse.

NAPOLEON (angrily sarcastic). Indeed! (With sudden misgiving.) Where are the letters and despatches?

THE LIEUTENANT (importantly, rather pleased than otherwise at having some remarkable news). I don't know.

NAPOLEON (unable to believe his ears). You don't know!

LIEUTENANT. No more than you do, General. Now I suppose I shall be court-martialled. Well, I don't mind being court-martialled; but (with solemn determination) I tell you, General, if ever I catch that innocent looking youth, I'll spoil his beauty, the slimy little liar! I'll make a picture of him. I'll—

NAPOLEON (advancing from the hearth to the table). What innocent looking youth? Pull yourself together, sir, will you; and give an account of yourself.

LIEUTENANT (facing him at the opposite side of the table, leaning on it with his fists). Oh, I'm all right, General: I'm perfectly ready to give an account of myself. I shall make the court-martial thoroughly understand that the fault was not mine. Advantage has been taken of the better side of my nature; and I'm not ashamed of it. But with all respect to you as my commanding officer, General, I say again that if ever I set eyes on that son of Satan, I'll—

NAPOLEON (angrily). So you said before.

LIEUTENANT (drawing himself upright). I say it again, just wait until I catch him. Just wait: that's all. (He folds his arms resolutely, and breathes hard, with compressed lips.)

NAPOLEON. I AM waiting, sir—for your explanation.

LIEUTENANT (confidently). You'll change your tone, General, when you hear what has happened to me.

NAPOLEON. Nothing has happened to you, sir: you are alive and not disabled. Where are the papers entrusted to you?

LIEUTENANT. Nothing! Nothing!! Oho! Well, we'll see. (Posing himself to overwhelm Napoleon with his news.) He swore eternal brotherhood with me. Was that nothing? He said my eyes reminded him of his sister's eyes. Was that nothing? He cried—actually cried—over the story of my separation from Angelica. Was that nothing? He paid for both bottles of wine, though he only ate bread and grapes himself. Perhaps you call that nothing! He gave me his pistols and his horse and his despatches—most important despatches—and let me go away with them. (Triumphantly, seeing that he has reduced Napoleon to blank stupefaction.) Was THAT nothing?

NAPOLEON (enfeebled by astonishment). What did he do that for?

LIEUTENANT (as if the reason were obvious). To show his confidence in me. (Napoleon's jaw does not exactly drop; but its hinges become nerveless. The Lieutenant proceeds with honest indignation.) And I was worthy of his confidence: I brought them all back honorably. But would you believe it?—when I trusted him with MY pistols, and MY horse, and MY despatches—

NAPOLEON (enraged). What the devil did you do that for?

LIEUTENANT. Why, to show my confidence in him, of course. And he betrayed it—abused it—never came back. The thief! the swindler! the heartless, treacherous little blackguard! You call that nothing, I suppose. But look here, General: (again resorting to the table with his fist for greater emphasis) YOU may put up with this outrage from the Austrians if you like; but speaking for myself personally, I tell you that if ever I catch—

NAPOLEON (turning on his heel in disgust and irritably resuming his march to and fro). Yes: you have said that more than once already.

LIEUTENANT (excitedly). More than once! I'll say it fifty times; and what's more, I'll do it. You'll see, General. I'll show my confidence in him, so I will. I'll—

NAPOLEON. Yes, yes, sir: no doubt you will. What kind of man was he?

LIEUTENANT. Well, I should think you ought to be able to tell from his conduct the sort of man he was.

NAPOLEON. Psh! What was he like?

LIEUTENANT. Like! He's like—well, you ought to have just seen the fellow: that will give you a notion of what he was like. He won't be like it five minutes after I catch him; for I tell you that if ever—

NAPOLEON (shouting furiously for the innkeeper). Giuseppe! (To the Lieutenant, out of all patience.) Hold your tongue, sir, if you can.

LIEUTENANT. I warn you it's no use to try to put the blame on me. (Plaintively.) How was I to know the sort of fellow he was? (He takes a chair from between the sideboard and the outer door; places it near the table; and sits down.) If you only knew how hungry and tired I am, you'd have more consideration.

GIUSEPPE (returning). What is it, excellency?

NAPOLEON (struggling with his temper). Take this—this officer. Feed him; and put him to bed, if necessary. When he is in his right mind again, find out what has happened to him and bring me word. (To the Lieutenant.) Consider yourself under arrest, sir.

LIEUTENANT (with sulky stiffness). I was prepared for that. It takes a gentleman to understand a gentleman. (He throws his sword on the table. Giuseppe takes it up and politely offers it to Napoleon, who throws it violently on the couch.)

GIUSEPPE (with sympathetic concern). Have you been attacked by the Austrians, lieutenant? Dear, dear, dear!

LIEUTENANT (contemptuously). Attacked! I could have broken his back between my finger and thumb. I wish I had, now. No: it was by appealing to the better side of my nature: that's what I can't get over. He said he'd never met a man he liked so much as me. He put his handkerchief round my neck because a gnat bit me, and my stock was chafing it. Look! (He pulls a handkerchief from his stock. Giuseppe takes it and examines it.)

GIUSEPPE (to Napoleon). A lady's handkerchief, excellency. (He smells it.) Perfumed!

NAPOLEON. Eh? (He takes it and looks at it attentively.) Hm! (He smells it.) Ha! (He walks thoughtfully across the room, looking at the handkerchief, which he finally sticks in the breast of his coat.)

LIEUTENANT. Good enough for him, anyhow. I noticed that he had a woman's hands when he touched my neck, with his coaxing, fawning ways, the mean, effeminate little hound. (Lowering his voice with thrilling intensity.) But mark my words, General. If ever—

THE LADY'S VOICE (outside, as before). Giuseppe!

LIEUTENANT (petrified). What was that?

GIUSEPPE. Only a lady upstairs, lieutenant, calling me.

LIEUTENANT. Lady!

VOICE. Giuseppe, Giuseppe: where ARE you?

LIEUTENANT (murderously). Give me that sword. (He strides to the couch; snatches the sword; and draws it.)

GIUSEPPE (rushing forward and seizing his right arm.) What are you thinking of, lieutenant? It's a lady: don't you hear that it's a woman's voice?

LIEUTENANT. It's HIS voice, I tell you. Let me go. (He breaks away, and rushes to the inner door. It opens in his face; and the Strange Lady steps in. She is a very attractive lady, tall and extraordinarily graceful, with a delicately intelligent, apprehensive, questioning face—perception in the brow, sensitiveness in the nostrils, character in the chin: all keen, refined, and original. She is very feminine, but by no means weak: the lithe, tender figure is hung on a strong frame: the hands and feet, neck and shoulders, are no fragile ornaments, but of full size in proportion to her stature, which considerably exceeds that of Napoleon and the innkeeper, and leaves her at no disadvantage with the lieutenant. Only her elegance and radiant charm keep the secret of her size and strength. She is not, judging by her dress, an admirer of the latest fashions of the Directory; or perhaps she uses up her old dresses for travelling. At all events she wears no jacket with extravagant lappels, no Greco-Tallien sham chiton, nothing, indeed, that the Princesse de Lamballe might not have worn. Her dress of flowered silk is long waisted, with a Watteau pleat behind, but with the paniers reduced to mere rudiments, as she is too tall for them. It is cut low in the neck, where it is eked out by a creamy fichu. She is fair, with golden brown hair and grey eyes.)

(She enters with the self-possession of a woman accustomed to the privileges of rank and beauty. The innkeeper, who has excellent natural manners, is highly appreciative of her. Napoleon, on whom her eyes first fall, is instantly smitten self-conscious. His color deepens: he becomes stiffer and less at ease than before. She perceives this instantly, and, not to embarrass him, turns in an infinitely well bred manner to pay the respect of a glance to the other gentleman, who is staring at her dress, as at the earth's final masterpiece of treacherous dissimulation, with feelings altogether inexpressible and indescribable. As she looks at him, she becomes deadly pale. There is no mistaking her expression: a revelation of some fatal error utterly unexpected, has suddenly appalled her in the midst of tranquillity, security and victory. The next moment a wave of color rushes up from beneath the creamy fichu and drowns her whole face. One can see that she is blushing all over her body. Even the lieutenant, ordinarily incapable of observation, and just now lost in the tumult of his wrath, can see a thing when it is painted red for him. Interpreting the blush as the involuntary confession of black deceit confronted with its victim, he points to it with a loud crow of retributive triumph, and then, seizing her by the wrist, pulls her past him into the room as he claps the door to, and plants himself with his back to it.)

LIEUTENANT. So I've got you, my lad. So you've disguised yourself, have you? (In a voice of thunder.) Take off that skirt.

GIUSEPPE (remonstrating). Oh, lieutenant!

LADY (affrighted, but highly indignant at his having dared to touch her). Gentlemen: I appeal to you. Giuseppe. (Making a movement as if to run to Giuseppe.)

LIEUTENANT (interposing, sword in hand). No you don't.

LADY (taking refuge with Napoleon). Ah, sir, you are an officer—a general. You will protect me, will you not?

LIEUTENANT. Never you mind him, General. Leave me to deal with him.

NAPOLEON. With him! With whom, sir? Why do you treat this lady in such a fashion?

LIEUTENANT. Lady! He's a man! the man I showed my confidence in. (Advancing threateningly.) Here you—

LADY (running behind Napoleon and in her agitation embracing the arm which he instinctively extends before her as a fortification). Oh, thank you, General. Keep him away.

NAPOLEON. Nonsense, sir. This is certainly a lady (she suddenly drops his arm and blushes again); and you are under arrest. Put down your sword, sir, instantly.

LIEUTENANT. General: I tell you he's an Austrian spy. He passed himself off on me as one of General Massena's staff this afternoon; and now he's passing himself off on you as a woman. Am I to believe my own eyes or not?

LADY. General: it must be my brother. He is on General Massena's staff. He is very like me.

LIEUTENANT (his mind giving way). Do you mean to say that you're not your brother, but your sister?—the sister who was so like me?—who had my beautiful blue eyes? It was a lie: your eyes are not like mine: they're exactly like your own. What perfidy!

NAPOLEON. Lieutenant: will you obey my orders and leave the room, since you are convinced at last that this is no gentleman?

LIEUTENANT. Gentleman! I should think not. No gentleman would have abused my confi—

NAPOLEON (out of all patience). Enough, sir, enough. Will you leave the room. I order you to leave the room.

LADY. Oh, pray let ME go instead.

NAPOLEON (drily). Excuse me, madame. With all respect to your brother, I do not yet understand what an officer on General Massena's staff wants with my letters. I have some questions to put to you.

GIUSEPPE (discreetly). Come, lieutenant. (He opens the door.)

LIEUTENANT. I'm off. General: take warning by me: be on your guard against the better side of your nature. (To the lady.)

Madame: my apologies. I thought you were the same person, only of the opposite sex; and that naturally misled me.

LADY (sweetly). It was not your fault, was it? I'm so glad you're not angry with me any longer, lieutenant. (She offers her hand.)

LIEUTENANT (bending gallantly to kiss it). Oh, madam, not the lea— (Checking himself and looking at it.) You have your brother's hand. And the same sort of ring.

LADY (sweetly). We are twins.

LIEUTENANT. That accounts for it. (He kisses her hand.) A thousand pardons. I didn't mind about the despatches at all: that's more the General's affair than mine: it was the abuse of my confidence through the better side of my nature. (Taking his cap, gloves, and whip from the table and going.) You'll excuse my leaving you, General, I hope. Very sorry, I'm sure. (He talks himself out of the room. Giuseppe follows him and shuts the door.)

NAPOLEON (looking after them with concentrated irritation). Idiot! (The Strange Lady smiles sympathetically. He comes frowning down the room between the table and the fireplace, all his awkwardness gone now that he is alone with her.)

LADY. How can I thank you, General, for your protection?

NAPOLEON (turning on her suddenly). My despatches: come! (He puts out his hand for them.)

LADY. General! (She involuntarily puts her hands on her fichu as if to protect something there.)

NAPOLEON. You tricked that blockhead out of them. You disguised yourself as a man. I want my despatches. They are there in the bosom of your dress, under your hands.

LADY (quickly removing her hands). Oh, how unkindly you are speaking to me! (She takes her handkerchief from her fichu.) You frighten me. (She touches her eyes as if to wipe away a tear.)

NAPOLEON. I see you don't know me madam, or you would save yourself the trouble of pretending to cry.

LADY (producing an effect of smiling through her tears). Yes, I do know you. You are the famous General Buonaparte. (She gives the name a marked Italian pronunciation Bwaw-na-parr-te.)

NAPOLEON (angrily, with the French pronunciation). Bonaparte, madame, Bonaparte. The papers, if you please.

LADY. But I assure you— (He snatches the handkerchief rudely from her.) General! (Indignantly.)

NAPOLEON (taking the other handkerchief from his breast). You were good enough to lend one of your handkerchiefs to my lieutenant when you robbed him. (He looks at the two handkerchiefs.) They match one another. (He smells them.) The same scent. (He flings them down on the table.) I am waiting for the despatches. I shall take them, if necessary, with as little ceremony as the handkerchief. (This historical incident was used eighty years later, by M. Victorien Sardou, in his drama entitled "Dora.")

LADY (in dignified reproof). General: do you threaten women?

NAPOLEON (bluntly). Yes.

LADY (disconcerted, trying to gain time). But I don't understand. I—

NAPOLEON. You understand perfectly. You came here because your Austrian employers calculated that I was six leagues away. I am always to be found where my enemies don't expect me. You have walked into the lion's den. Come: you are a brave woman. Be a sensible one: I have no time to waste. The papers. (He advances a step ominously).

LADY (breaking down in the childish rage of impotence, and throwing herself in tears on the chair left beside the table by the lieutenant). I brave! How little you know! I have spent the day in an agony of fear. I have a pain here from the tightening of my heart at every suspicious look, every threatening movement. Do you think every one is as brave as you? Oh, why will not you brave people do the brave things? Why do you leave them to us, who have no courage at all? I'm not brave: I shrink from violence: danger makes me miserable.

NAPOLEON (interested). Then why have you thrust yourself into danger?

LADY. Because there is no other way: I can trust nobody else. And now it is all useless—all because of you, who have no fear, because you have no heart, no feeling, no— (She breaks off, and throws herself on her knees.) Ah, General, let me go: let me go without asking any questions. You shall have your despatches and letters: I swear it.

NAPOLEON (holding out his hand). Yes: I am waiting for them. (She gasps, daunted by his ruthless promptitude into despair of moving him by cajolery; but as she looks up perplexedly at him, it is plain that she is racking her brains for some device to outwit him. He meets her regard inflexibly.)

LADY (rising at last with a quiet little sigh). I will get them for you. They are in my room. (She turns to the door.)

NAPOLEON. I shall accompany you, madame.

LADY (drawing herself up with a noble air of offended delicacy).I cannot permit you, General, to enter my chamber.

NAPOLEON. Then you shall stay here, madame, whilst I have your chamber searched for my papers.

LADY (spitefully, openly giving up her plan). You may save yourself the trouble. They are not there.

NAPOLEON. No: I have already told you where they are. (Pointing to her breast.)

LADY (with pretty piteousness). General: I only want to keep one little private letter. Only one. Let me have it.

NAPOLEON (cold and stern). Is that a reasonable demand, madam?

LADY (encouraged by his not refusing point blank). No; but that is why you must grant it. Are your own demands reasonable? thousands of lives for the sake of your victories, your ambitions, your destiny! And what I ask is such a little thing. And I am only a weak woman, and you a brave man. (She looks at him with her eyes full of tender pleading and is about to kneel to him again.)

NAPOLEON (brusquely). Get up, get up. (He turns moodily away and takes a turn across the room, pausing for a moment to say, over his shoulder) You're talking nonsense; and you know it. (She gets up and sits down in almost listless despair on the couch. When he turns and sees her there, he feels that his victory is complete, and that he may now indulge in a little play with his victim. He comes back and sits beside her. She looks alarmed and moves a little away from him; but a ray of rallying hope beams from her eye. He begins like a man enjoying some secret joke.) How do you know I am a brave man?

LADY (amazed). You! General Buonaparte. (Italian pronunciation.)

NAPOLEON. Yes, I, General Bonaparte (emphasizing the French pronunciation).

LADY. Oh, how can you ask such a question? you! who stood only two days ago at the bridge at Lodi, with the air full of death, fighting a duel with cannons across the river! (Shuddering.) Oh, you DO brave things.

NAPOLEON. So do you.

LADY. I! (With a sudden odd thought.) Oh! Are you a coward?

NAPOLEON (laughing grimly and pinching her cheek). That is the one question you must never ask a soldier. The sergeant asks after the recruit's height, his age, his wind, his limb, but never after his courage. (He gets up and walks about with his hands behind him and his head bowed, chuckling to himself.)

LADY (as if she had found it no laughing matter). Ah, you can laugh at fear. Then you don't know what fear is.

NAPOLEON (coming behind the couch). Tell me this. Suppose you could have got that letter by coming to me over the bridge at Lodi the day before yesterday! Suppose there had been no other way, and that this was a sure way—if only you escaped the cannon! (She shudders and covers her eyes for a moment with her hands.) Would you have been afraid?

LADY. Oh, horribly afraid, agonizingly afraid. (She presses her hands on her heart.) It hurts only to imagine it.

NAPOLEON (inflexibly). Would you have come for the despatches?

LADY (overcome by the imagined horror). Don't ask me. I must have come.

NAPOLEON. Why?

LADY. Because I must. Because there would have been no other way.

NAPOLEON (with conviction). Because you would have wanted my letter enough to bear your fear. There is only one universal passion: fear. Of all the thousand qualities a man may have, the only one you will find as certainly in the youngest drummer boy in my army as in me, is fear. It is fear that makes men fight: it is indifference that makes them run away: fear is the mainspring of war. Fear! I know fear well, better than you, better than any woman. I once saw a regiment of good Swiss soldiers massacred by a mob in Paris because I was afraid to interfere: I felt myself a coward to the tips of my toes as I looked on at it. Seven months ago I revenged my shame by pounding that mob to death with cannon balls. Well, what of that? Has fear ever held a man back from anything he really wanted—or a woman either? Never. Come with me; and I will show you twenty thousand cowards who will risk death every day for the price of a glass of brandy. And do you think there are no women in the army, braver than the men, because their lives are worth less? Psha! I think nothing of your fear or your bravery. If you had had to come across to me at Lodi, you would not have been afraid: once on the bridge, every other feeling would have gone down before the necessity—the necessity—for making your way to my side and getting what you wanted.

And now, suppose you had done all this—suppose you had come safely out with that letter in your hand, knowing that when the hour came, your fear had tightened, not your heart, but your grip of your own purpose—that it had ceased to be fear, and had become strength, penetration, vigilance, iron resolution—how would you answer then if you were asked whether you were a coward?

LADY (rising). Ah, you are a hero, a real hero.

NAPOLEON. Pooh! there's no such thing as a real hero. (He strolls down the room, making light of her enthusiasm, but by no means displeased with himself for having evoked it.)

LADY. Ah, yes, there is. There is a difference between what you call my bravery and yours. You wanted to win the battle of Lodi for yourself and not for anyone else, didn't you?

NAPOLEON. Of course. (Suddenly recollecting himself.) Stop: no. (He pulls himself piously together, and says, like a man conducting a religious service) I am only the servant of the French republic, following humbly in the footsteps of the heroes of classical antiquity. I win battles for humanity—for my country, not for myself.

LADY (disappointed). Oh, then you are only a womanish hero, after all. (She sits down again, all her enthusiasm gone, her elbow on the end of the couch, and her cheek propped on her hand.)

NAPOLEON (greatly astonished). Womanish!

LADY (listlessly). Yes, like me. (With deep melancholy.) Do you think that if I only wanted those despatches for myself, I dare venture into a battle for them? No: if that were all, I should not have the courage to ask to see you at your hotel, even. My courage is mere slavishness: it is of no use to me for my own purposes. It is only through love, through pity, through the instinct to save and protect someone else, that I can do the things that terrify me.

NAPOLEON (contemptuously). Pshaw! (He turns slightingly away from her.)

LADY. Aha! now you see that I'm not really brave. (Relapsing into petulant listlessness.) But what right have you to despise me if you only win your battles for others? for your country! through patriotism! That is what I call womanish: it is so like a Frenchman!

NAPOLEON (furiously). I am no Frenchman.

LADY (innocently). I thought you said you won the battle of Lodi for your country, General Bu— shall I pronounce it in Italian or French?

NAPOLEON. You are presuming on my patience, madam. I was born a French subject, but not in France.

LADY (folding her arms on the end of the couch, and leaning on them with a marked access of interest in him). You were not born a subject at all, I think.

NAPOLEON (greatly pleased, starting on a fresh march). Eh? Eh? You think not.

LADY. I am sure of it.

NAPOLEON. Well, well, perhaps not. (The self-complacency of his assent catches his own ear. He stops short, reddening. Then, composing himself into a solemn attitude, modelled on the heroes of classical antiquity, he takes a high moral tone.) But we must not live for ourselves alone, little one. Never forget that we should always think of others, and work for others, and lead and govern them for their own good. Self-sacrifice is the foundation of all true nobility of character.

LADY (again relaxing her attitude with a sigh). Ah, it is easy to see that you have never tried it, General.

NAPOLEON (indignantly, forgetting all about Brutus and Scipio). What do you mean by that speech, madam?

LADY. Haven't you noticed that people always exaggerate the value of the things they haven't got? The poor think they only need riches to be quite happy and good. Everybody worships truth, purity, unselfishness, for the same reason—because they have no experience of them. Oh, if they only knew!

NAPOLEON (with angry derision). If they only knew! Pray, do you know?

LADY (with her arms stretched down and her hands clasped on her knees, looking straight before her). Yes. I had the misfortune to be born good. (Glancing up at him for a moment.) And it is a misfortune, I can tell you, General. I really am truthful and unselfish and all the rest of it; and it's nothing but cowardice; want of character; want of being really, strongly, positively oneself.

NAPOLEON. Ha? (Turning to her quickly with a flash of strong interest.)

LADY (earnestly, with rising enthusiasm). What is the secret of your power? Only that you believe in yourself. You can fight and conquer for yourself and for nobody else. You are not afraid of your own destiny. You teach us what we all might be if we had the will and courage; and that (suddenly sinking on her knees before him) is why we all begin to worship you. (She kisses his hands.)

NAPOLEON (embarrassed). Tut, tut! Pray rise, madam.

LADY. Do not refuse my homage: it is your right. You will be emperor of France.

NAPOLEON (hurriedly). Take care. Treason!

LADY (insisting). Yes, emperor of France; then of Europe; perhaps of the world. I am only the first subject to swear allegiance. (Again kissing his hand.) My Emperor!

NAPOLEON (overcome, raising her). Pray, pray. No, no, little one: this is folly. Come: be calm, be calm. (Petting her.) There, there, my girl.

LADY (struggling with happy tears). Yes, I know it is an impertinence in me to tell you what you must know far better than I do. But you are not angry with me, are you?

NAPOLEON. Angry! No, no: not a bit, not a bit. Come: you are a very clever and sensible and interesting little woman. (He pats her on the cheek.) Shall we be friends?

LADY (enraptured). Your friend! You will let me be your friend! Oh! (She offers him both her hands with a radiant smile.) You see: I show my confidence in you.

NAPOLEON (with a yell of rage, his eyes flashing). What!

LADY. What's the matter?

NAPOLEON. Show your confidence in me! So that I may show my confidence in you in return by letting you give me the slip with the despatches, eh? Ah, Dalila, Dalila, you have been trying your tricks on me; and I have been as great a gull as my jackass of a lieutenant. (He advances threateningly on her.) Come: the despatches. Quick: I am not to be trifled with now.

LADY (flying round the couch). General—

NAPOLEON. Quick, I tell you. (He passes swiftly up the middle of the room and intercepts her as she makes for the vineyard.)

LADY (at bay, confronting him). You dare address me in that tone.

NAPOLEON. Dare!

LADY. Yes, dare. Who are you that you should presume to speak to me in that coarse way? Oh, the vile, vulgar Corsican adventurer comes out in you very easily.

NAPOLEON (beside himself). You she devil! (Savagely.) Once more, and only once, will you give me those papers or shall I tear them from you—by force?

LADY (letting her hands fall). Tear them from me—by force! (As he glares at her like a tiger about to spring, she crosses her arms on her breast in the attitude of a martyr. The gesture and pose instantly awaken his theatrical instinct: he forgets his rage in the desire to show her that in acting, too, she has met her match. He keeps her a moment in suspense; then suddenly clears up his countenance; puts his hands behind him with provoking coolness; looks at her up and down a couple of times; takes a pinch of snuff; wipes his fingers carefully and puts up his handkerchief, her heroic pose becoming more and more ridiculous all the time.)

NAPOLEON (at last). Well?

LADY (disconcerted, but with her arms still crossed devotedly). Well: what are you going to do?

NAPOLEON. Spoil your attitude.

LADY. You brute! (abandoning the attitude, she comes to the end of the couch, where she turns with her back to it, leaning against it and facing him with her hands behind her.)

NAPOLEON. Ah, that's better. Now listen to me. I like you. What's more, I value your respect.

LADY. You value what you have not got, then.

NAPOLEON. I shall have it presently. Now attend to me. Suppose I were to allow myself to be abashed by the respect due to your sex, your beauty, your heroism and all the rest of it? Suppose I, with nothing but such sentimental stuff to stand between these muscles of mine and those papers which you have about you, and which I want and mean to have: suppose I, with the prize within my grasp, were to falter and sneak away with my hands empty; or, what would be worse, cover up my weakness by playing the magnanimous hero, and sparing you the violence I dared not use, would you not despise me from the depths of your woman's soul? Would any woman be such a fool? Well, Bonaparte can rise to the situation and act like a woman when it is necessary. Do you understand?

The lady, without speaking, stands upright, and takes a packet of papers from her bosom. For a moment she has an intense impulse to dash them in his face. But her good breeding cuts her off from any vulgar method of relief. She hands them to him politely, only averting her head. The moment he takes them, she hurries across to the other side of the room; covers her face with her hands; and sits down, with her body turned away to the back of the chair.

NAPOLEON (gloating over the papers). Aha! That's right. That's right. (Before opening them he looks at her and says) Excuse me. (He sees that she is hiding her face.) Very angry with me, eh? (He unties the packet, the seal of which is already broken, and puts it on the table to examine its contents.)

LADY (quietly, taking down her hands and showing that she is not crying, but only thinking). No. You were right. But I am sorry for you.

NAPOLEON (pausing in the act of taking the uppermost paper from the packet). Sorry for me! Why?

LADY. I am going to see you lose your honor.

NAPOLEON. Hm! Nothing worse than that? (He takes up the paper.)

LADY. And your happiness.

NAPOLEON. Happiness, little woman, is the most tedious thing in the world to me. Should I be what I am if I cared for happiness? Anything else?

LADY. Nothing— (He interrupts her with an exclamation of satisfaction. She proceeds quietly) except that you will cut a very foolish figure in the eyes of France.

NAPOLEON (quickly). What? (The hand holding the paper involuntarily drops. The lady looks at him enigmatically in tranquil silence. He throws the letter down and breaks out into a torrent of scolding.) What do you mean? Eh? Are you at your tricks again? Do you think I don't know what these papers contain? I'll tell you. First, my information as to Beaulieu's retreat. There are only two things he can do—leatherbrained idiot that he is!—shut himself up in Mantua or violate the neutrality of Venice by taking Peschiera. You are one of old Leatherbrain's spies: he has discovered that he has been betrayed, and has sent you to intercept the information at all hazards—as if that could save him from ME, the old fool! The other papers are only my usual correspondence from Paris, of which you know nothing.

LADY (prompt and businesslike). General: let us make a fair division. Take the information your spies have sent you about the Austrian army; and give me the Paris correspondence. That will content me.

NAPOLEON (his breath taken away by the coolness of the proposal). A fair di— (He gasps.) It seems to me, madame, that you have come to regard my letters as your own property, of which I am trying to rob you.

LADY (earnestly). No: on my honor I ask for no letter of yours—not a word that has been written by you or to you. That packet contains a stolen letter: a letter written by a woman to a man—a man not her husband—a letter that means disgrace, infamy—

NAPOLEON. A love letter?

LADY (bitter-sweetly). What else but a love letter could stir up so much hate?

NAPOLEON. Why is it sent to me? To put the husband in my power, eh?

LADY. No, no: it can be of no use to you: I swear that it will cost you nothing to give it to me. It has been sent to you out of sheer malice—solely to injure the woman who wrote it.

NAPOLEON. Then why not send it to her husband instead of to me?

LADY (completely taken aback). Oh! (Sinking back into the chair.) I—I don't know. (She breaks down.)

NAPOLEON. Aha! I thought so: a little romance to get the papers back. (He throws the packet on the table and confronts her with cynical goodhumor.) Per Bacco, little woman, I can't help admiring you. If I could lie like that, it would save me a great deal of trouble.

LADY (wringing her hands). Oh, how I wish I really had told you some lie! You would have believed me then. The truth is the one thing that nobody will believe.

NAPOLEON (with coarse familiarity, treating her as if she were a vivandiere). Capital! Capital! (He puts his hands behind him on the table, and lifts himself on to it, sitting with his arms akimbo and his legs wide apart.) Come: I am a true Corsican in my love for stories. But I could tell them better than you if I set my mind to it. Next time you are asked why a letter compromising a wife should not be sent to her husband, answer simply that the husband would not read it. Do you suppose, little innocent, that a man wants to be compelled by public opinion to make a scene, to fight a duel, to break up his household, to injure his career by a scandal, when he can avoid it all by taking care not to know?

LADY (revolted). Suppose that packet contained a letter about your own wife?

NAPOLEON (offended, coming off the table). You are impertinent, madame.

LADY (humbly). I beg your above suspicion.

NAPOLEON (with a deliberate assumption of superiority). You have committed an indiscretion. I pardon you. In future, do not permit yourself to introduce real persons in your romances.

LADY (politely ignoring a speech which is to her only a breach of good manners, and rising to move towards the table). General: there really is a woman's letter there. (Pointing to the packet.) Give it to me.

NAPOLEON (with brute conciseness, moving so as to prevent her getting too near the letters). Why?

LADY. She is an old friend: we were at school together. She has written to me imploring me to prevent the letter falling into your hands.

NAPOLEON. Why has it been sent to me?

LADY. Because it compromises the director Barras.

NAPOLEON (frowning, evidently startled). Barras! (Haughtily.) Take care, madame. The director Barras is my attached personal friend.

LADY (nodding placidly). Yes. You became friends through your wife.

NAPOLEON. Again! Have I not forbidden you to speak of my wife? (She keeps looking curiously at him, taking no account of the rebuke. More and more irritated, he drops his haughty manner, of which he is himself somewhat impatient, and says suspiciously, lowering his voice) Who is this woman with whom you sympathize so deeply?

LADY. Oh, General! How could I tell you that?

NAPOLEON (ill-humoredly, beginning to walk about again in angry perplexity). Ay, ay: stand by one another. You are all the same, you women.

LADY (indignantly). We are not all the same, any more than you are. Do you think that if *I* loved another man, I should pretend to go on loving my husband, or be afraid to tell him or all the world? But this woman is not made that way. She governs men by cheating them; and (with disdain) they like it, and let her govern them. (She sits down again, with her back to him.)

NAPOLEON (not attending to her). Barras, Barras I— (Turning very threateningly to her, his face darkening.) Take care, take care: do you hear? You may go too far.

LADY (innocently turning her face to him). What's the matter?

NAPOLEON. What are you hinting at? Who is this woman?

LADY (meeting his angry searching gaze with tranquil indifference as she sits looking up at him with her right arm resting lightly along the back of her chair, and one knee crossed over the other). A vain, silly, extravagant creature, with a very able and ambitious husband who knows her through and through—knows that she has lied to him about her age, her income, her social position, about everything that silly women lie about—knows that she is incapable of fidelity to any principle or any person; and yet could not help loving her—could not help his man's instinct to make use of her for his own advancement with Barras.

NAPOLEON (in a stealthy, coldly furious whisper). This is your revenge, you she cat, for having had to give me the letters.

LADY. Nonsense! Or do you mean that YOU are that sort of man?

NAPOLEON (exasperated, clasps his hands behind him, his fingers twitching, and says, as he walks irritably away from her to the fireplace). This woman will drive me out of my senses. (To her.) Begone.

LADY (seated immovably). Not without that letter.

NAPOLEON. Begone, I tell you. (Walking from the fireplace to the vineyard and back to the table.) You shall have no letter. I don't like you. You're a detestable woman, and as ugly as Satan. I don't choose to be pestered by strange women. Be off. (He turns his back on her. In quiet amusement, she leans her cheek on her hand and laughs at him. He turns again, angrily mocking her.) Ha! ha! ha! What are you laughing at?

LADY. At you, General. I have often seen persons of your sex getting into a pet and behaving like children; but I never saw a really great man do it before.

NAPOLEON (brutally, flinging the words in her face). Pooh: flattery! flattery! coarse, impudent flattery!

LADY (springing up with a bright flush in her cheeks). Oh, you are too bad. Keep your letters. Read the story of your own dishonor in them; and much good may they do you. Good-bye. (She goes indignantly towards the inner door.)

NAPOLEON. My own—! Stop. Come back. Come back, I order you. (She proudly disregards his savagely peremptory tone and continues on her way to the door. He rushes at her; seizes her by the wrist; and drags her back.) Now, what do you mean? Explain. Explain, I tell you, or—(Threatening her. She looks at him with unflinching defiance.) Rrrr! you obstinate devil, you. Why can't you answer a civil question?

LADY (deeply offended by his violence). Why do you ask me? You have the explanation.

NAPOLEON. Where?

LADY (pointing to the letters on the table). There. You have only to read it. (He snatches the packet up, hesitates; looks at her suspiciously; and throws it down again.)

NAPOLEON. You seem to have forgotten your solicitude for the honor of your old friend.

LADY. She runs no risk now: she does not quite understand her husband.

NAPOLEON. I am to read the letter, then? (He stretches out his hand as if to take up the packet again, with his eye on her.)

LADY. I do not see how you can very well avoid doing so now. (He instantly withdraws his hand.) Oh, don't be afraid. You will find many interesting things in it.

NAPOLEON. For instance?

LADY. For instance, a duel—with Barras, a domestic scene, a broken household, a public scandal, a checked career, all sorts of things.

NAPOLEON. Hm! (He looks at her, takes up the packet and looks at it, pursing his lips and balancing it in his hand; looks at her again; passes the packet into his left hand and puts it behind his back, raising his right to scratch the back of his head as he turns and goes up to the edge of the vineyard, where he stands for a moment looking out into the vines, deep in thought. The Lady watches him in silence, somewhat slightingly. Suddenly he turns and comes back again, full of force and decision.) I grant your request, madame. Your courage and resolution deserve to succeed. Take the letters for which you have fought so well; and remember henceforth that you found the vile, vulgar Corsican adventurer as generous to the vanquished after the battle as he was resolute in the face of the enemy before it. (He offers her the packet.)

LADY (without taking it, looking hard at him). What are you at now, I wonder? (He dashes the packet furiously to the floor.) Aha! I've spoiled that attitude, I think. (She makes him a pretty mocking curtsey.)

NAPOLEON (snatching it up again). Will you take the letters and begone (advancing and thrusting them upon her)?

LADY (escaping round the table). No: I don't want letters.

NAPOLEON. Ten minutes ago, nothing else would satisfy you.

LADY (keeping the table carefully between them). Ten minutes ago you had not insulted me past all bearing.

NAPOLEON. I— (swallowing his spleen) I apologize.

LADY (coolly). Thanks. (With forced politeness he offers her the packet across the table. She retreats a step out of its reach and says) But don't you want to know whether the Austrians are at Mantua or Peschiera?

NAPOLEON. I have already told you that I can conquer my enemies without the aid of spies, madame.

LADY. And the letter! don't you want to read that?

NAPOLEON. You have said that it is not addressed to me. I am not in the habit of reading other people's letters. (He again offers the packet.)

LADY. In that case there can be no objection to your keeping it. All I wanted was to prevent your reading it. (Cheerfully.) Good afternoon, General. (She turns coolly towards the inner door.)

NAPOLEON (furiously flinging the packet on the couch). Heaven grant me patience! (He goes up determinedly and places himself before the door.) Have you any sense of personal danger? Or are you one of those women who like to be beaten black and blue?

LADY. Thank you, General: I have no doubt the sensation is very voluptuous; but I had rather not. I simply want to go home: that's all. I was wicked enough to steal your despatches; but you have got them back; and you have forgiven me, because (delicately reproducing his rhetorical cadence) you are as generous to the vanquished after the battle as you are resolute in the face of the enemy before it. Won't you say good-bye to me? (She offers her hand sweetly.)

NAPOLEON (repulsing the advance with a gesture of concentrated rage, and opening the door to call fiercely). Giuseppe! (Louder.) Giuseppe! (He bangs the door to, and comes to the middle of the room. The lady goes a little way into the vineyard to avoid him.)

GIUSEPPE (appearing at the door). Excellency?

NAPOLEON. Where is that fool?

GIUSEPPE. He has had a good dinner, according to your instructions, excellency, and is now doing me the honor to gamble with me to pass the time.

NAPOLEON. Send him here. Bring him here. Come with him. (Giuseppe, with unruffled readiness, hurries off. Napoleon turns curtly to the lady, saying) I must trouble you to remain some moments longer, madame. (He comes to the couch. She comes from the vineyard down the opposite side of the room to the sideboard, and posts herself there, leaning against it, watching him. He takes the packet from the couch and deliberately buttons it carefully into his breast pocket, looking at her meanwhile with an expression which suggests that she will soon find out the meaning of his proceedings, and will not like it. Nothing more is said until the lieutenant arrives followed by Giuseppe, who stands modestly in attendance at the table. The lieutenant, without cap, sword or gloves, and much improved in temper and spirits by his meal, chooses the Lady's side of the room, and waits, much at his ease, for Napoleon to begin.)

NAPOLEON. Lieutenant.

LIEUTENANT (encouragingly). General.

NAPOLEON. I cannot persuade this lady to give me much information; but there can be no doubt that the man who tricked you out of your charge was, as she admitted to you, her brother.

LIEUTENANT (triumphantly). What did I tell you, General! What did I tell you!

NAPOLEON. You must find that man. Your honor is at stake; and the fate of the campaign, the destiny of France, of Europe, of humanity, perhaps, may depend on the information those despatches contain.

LIEUTENANT. Yes, I suppose they really are rather serious (as if this had hardly occurred to him before).

NAPOLEON (energetically). They are so serious, sir, that if you do not recover them, you will be degraded in the presence of your regiment.

LIEUTENANT. Whew! The regiment won't like that, I can tell you.

NAPOLEON. Personally, I am sorry for you. I would willingly conceal the affair if it were possible. But I shall be called to account for not acting on the despatches. I shall have to prove to all the world that I never received them, no matter what the consequences may be to you. I am sorry; but you see that I cannot help myself.

LIEUTENANT (goodnaturedly). Oh, don't take it to heart, General: it's really very good of you. Never mind what happens to me: I shall scrape through somehow; and we'll beat the Austrians for you, despatches or no despatches. I hope you won't insist on my starting off on a wild goose chase after the fellow now. I haven't a notion where to look for him.

GIUSEPPE (deferentially). You forget, Lieutenant: he has your horse.

LIEUTENANT (starting). I forgot that. (Resolutely.) I'll go after him, General: I'll find that horse if it's alive anywhere in Italy. And I shan't forget the despatches: never fear. Giuseppe: go and saddle one of those mangy old posthorses of yours, while I get my cap and sword and things. Quick march. Off with you (bustling him).

GIUSEPPE. Instantly, Lieutenant, instantly. (He disappears in the vineyard, where the light is now reddening with the sunset.)

LIEUTENANT (looking about him on his way to the inner door). By the way, General, did I give you my sword or did I not? Oh, I remember now. (Fretfully.) It's all that nonsense about putting a man under arrest: one never knows where to find— (Talks himself out of the room.)

LADY (still at the sideboard). What does all this mean, General?

NAPOLEON. He will not find your brother.

LADY. Of course not. There's no such person.

NAPOLEON. The despatches will be irrecoverably lost.

LADY. Nonsense! They are inside your coat.

NAPOLEON. You will find it hard, I think, to prove that wild statement. (The Lady starts. He adds, with clinching emphasis) Those papers are lost.

LADY (anxiously, advancing to the corner of the table). And that unfortunate young man's career will be sacrificed.

NAPOLEON. HIS career! The fellow is not worth the gunpowder it would cost to have him shot. (He turns contemptuously and goes to the hearth, where he stands with his back to her.)

LADY (wistfully). You are very hard. Men and women are nothing to you but things to be used, even if they are broken in the use.

NAPOLEON (turning on her). Which of us has broken this fellow—I or you? Who tricked him out of the despatches? Did you think of his career then?

LADY (naively concerned about him). Oh, I never thought of that. It was brutal of me; but I couldn't help it, could I? How else could I have got the papers? (Supplicating.) General: you will save him from disgrace.

NAPOLEON (laughing sourly). Save him yourself, since you are so clever: it was you who ruined him. (With savage intensity.) I HATE a bad soldier.

He goes out determinedly through the vineyard. She follows him a few steps with an appealing gesture, but is interrupted by the return of the lieutenant, gloved and capped, with his sword on, ready for the road. He is crossing to the outer door when she intercepts him.

LADY. Lieutenant.

LIEUTENANT (importantly). You mustn't delay me, you know. Duty, madame, duty.

LADY (imploringly). Oh, sir, what are you going to do to my poor brother?

LIEUTENANT. Are you very fond of him?

LADY. I should die if anything happened to him. You must spare him. (The lieutenant shakes his head gloomily.) Yes, yes: you must: you shall: he is not fit to die. Listen to me. If I tell you where to find him—if I undertake to place him in your hands a prisoner, to be delivered up by you to General Bonaparte—will you promise me on your honor as an officer and a gentleman not to fight with him or treat him unkindly in any way?

LIEUTENANT. But suppose he attacks me. He has my pistols.

LADY. He is too great a coward.

LIEUTENANT. I don't feel so sure about that. He's capable of anything.

LADY. If he attacks you, or resists you in any way, I release you from your promise.

LIEUTENANT. My promise! I didn't mean to promise. Look here: you're as bad as he is: you've taken an advantage of me through the better side of my nature. What about my horse?

LADY. It is part of the bargain that you are to have your horse and pistols back.

LIEUTENANT. Honor bright?

LADY. Honor bright. (She offers her hand.)

LIEUTENANT (taking it and holding it). All right: I'll be as gentle as a lamb with him. His sister's a very pretty woman. (He attempts to kiss her.)

LADY (slipping away from him). Oh, Lieutenant! You forget: your career is at stake—the destiny of Europe—of humanity.

LIEUTENANT. Oh, bother the destiny of humanity (Making for her.) Only a kiss.

LADY (retreating round the table). Not until you have regained your honor as an officer. Remember: you have not captured my brother yet.

LIEUTENANT (seductively). You'll tell me where he is, won't you?

LADY. I have only to send him a certain signal; and he will be here in quarter of an hour.

LIEUTENANT. He's not far off, then.

LADY. No: quite close. Wait here for him: when he gets my message he will come here at once and surrender himself to you. You understand?

LIEUTENANT (intellectually overtaxed). Well, it's a little complicated; but I daresay it will be all right.

LADY. And now, whilst you're waiting, don't you think you had better make terms with the General?

LIEUTENANT. Oh, look here, this is getting frightfully complicated. What terms?

LADY. Make him promise that if you catch my brother he will consider that you have cleared your character as a soldier. He will promise anything you ask on that condition.

LIEUTENANT. That's not a bad idea. Thank you: I think I'll try it.

LADY. Do. And mind, above all things, don't let him see how clever you are.

LIEUTENANT. I understand. He'd be jealous.

LADY. Don't tell him anything except that you are resolved to capture my brother or perish in the attempt. He won't believe you. Then you will produce my brother—

LIEUTENANT (interrupting as he masters the plot). And have the laugh at him! I say: what a clever little woman you are! (Shouting.) Giuseppe!

LADY. Sh! Not a word to Giuseppe about me. (She puts her finger on her lips. He does the same. They look at one another warningly. Then, with a ravishing smile, she changes the gesture into wafting him a kiss, and runs out through the inner door. Electrified, he bursts into a volley of chuckles. Giuseppe comes back by the outer door.)

GIUSEPPE. The horse is ready, Lieutenant.

LIEUTENANT. I'm not going just yet. Go and find the General, and tell him I want to speak to him.

GIUSEPPE (shaking his head). That will never do, Lieutenant.

LIEUTENANT. Why not?

GIUSEPPE. In this wicked world a general may send for a lieutenant; but a lieutenant must not send for a general.

LIEUTENANT. Oh, you think he wouldn't like it. Well, perhaps you're right: one has to be awfully particular about that sort of thing now we've got a republic.

Napoleon reappears, advancing from the vineyard, buttoning the breast of his coat, pale and full of gnawing thoughts.

GIUSEPPE (unconscious of Napoleon's approach). Quite true, Lieutenant, quite true. You are all like innkeepers now in France: you have to be polite to everybody.

NAPOLEON (putting his hand on Giuseppe's shoulder). And that destroys the whole value of politeness, eh?

LIEUTENANT. The very man I wanted! See here, General: suppose I catch that fellow for you!

NAPOLEON (with ironical gravity). You will not catch him, my friend.

LIEUTENANT. Aha! you think so; but you'll see. Just wait. Only, if I do catch him and hand him over to you, will you cry quits? Will you drop all this about degrading me in the presence of my regiment? Not that I mind, you know; but still no regiment likes to have all the other regiments laughing at it.

NAPOLEON. (a cold ray of humor striking pallidly across his gloom). What shall we do with this officer, Giuseppe? Everything he says is wrong.

GIUSEPPE (promptly). Make him a general, excellency; and then everything he says will be right.

LIEUTENANT (crowing). Haw-aw! (He throws himself ecstatically on the couch to enjoy the joke.)

NAPOLEON (laughing and pinching Giuseppe's ear). You are thrown away in this inn, Giuseppe. (He sits down and places Giuseppe before him like a schoolmaster with a pupil.) Shall I take you away with me and make a man of you?

GIUSEPPE (shaking his head rapidly and repeatedly). No, thank you, General. All my life long people have wanted to make a man of me. When I was a boy, our good priest wanted to make a man of me by teaching me to read and write. Then the organist at Melegnano wanted to make a man of me by teaching me to read music. The recruiting sergeant would have made a man of me if I had been a few inches taller. But it always meant making me work; and I am too lazy for that, thank Heaven! So I taught myself to cook and became an innkeeper; and now I keep servants to do the work, and have nothing to do myself except talk, which suits me perfectly.

NAPOLEON (looking at him thoughtfully). You are satisfied?

GIUSEPPE (with cheerful conviction). Quite, excellency.

NAPOLEON. And you have no devouring devil inside you who must be fed with action and victory—gorged with them night and day—who makes you pay, with the sweat of your brain and body, weeks of Herculean toil for ten minutes of enjoyment—who is at once your slave and your tyrant, your genius and your doom—who brings you a crown in one hand and the oar of a galley slave in the other—who shows you all the kingdoms of the earth and offers to make you their master on condition that you become their servant!—have you nothing of that in you?

GIUSEPPE. Nothing of it! Oh, I assure you, excellency, MY devouring devil is far worse than that. He offers me no crowns and kingdoms: he expects to get everything for nothing—sausages, omelettes, grapes, cheese, polenta, wine—three times a day, excellency: nothing less will content him.

LIEUTENANT. Come, drop it, Giuseppe: you're making me feel hungry again.

(Giuseppe, with an apologetic shrug, retires from the conversation, and busies himself at the table, dusting it, setting the map straight, and replacing Napoleon's chair, which the lady has pushed back.)

NAPOLEON (turning to the lieutenant with sardonic ceremony). I hope *I* have not been making you feel ambitious.

LIEUTENANT. Not at all: I don't fly so high. Besides: I'm better as I am: men like me are wanted in the army just now. The fact is, the Revolution was all very well for civilians; but it won't work in the army. You know what soldiers are, General: they WILL have men of family for their officers. A subaltern must be a gentleman, because he's so much in contact with the men. But a general, or even a colonel, may be any sort of riff-raff if he understands the shop well enough. A lieutenant is a gentleman: all the rest is chance. Why, who do you suppose won the battle of Lodi? I'll tell you. My horse did.

NAPOLEON (rising) Your folly is carrying you too far, sir. Take care.

LIEUTENANT. Not a bit of it. You remember all that red-hot cannonade across the river: the Austrians blazing away at you to keep you from crossing, and you blazing away at them to keep them from setting the bridge on fire? Did you notice where I was then?

NAPOLEON (with menacing politeness). I am sorry. I am afraid I was rather occupied at the moment.

GIUSEPPE (with eager admiration). They say you jumped off your horse and worked the big guns with your own hands, General.

LIEUTENANT. That was a mistake: an officer should never let himself down to the level of his men. (Napoleon looks at him dangerously, and begins to walk tigerishly to and fro.) But you might have been firing away at the Austrians still, if we cavalry fellows hadn't found the ford and got across and turned old Beaulieu's flank for you. You know you daren't have given the order to charge the bridge if you hadn't seen us on the other side. Consequently, I say that whoever found that ford won the battle of Lodi. Well, who found it? I was the first man to cross: and I know. It was my horse that found it. (With conviction, as he rises from the couch.) That horse is the true conqueror of the Austrians.

NAPOLEON (passionately). You idiot: I'll have you shot for losing those despatches: I'll have you blown from the mouth of a cannon: nothing less could make any impression on you. (Baying at him.) Do you hear? Do you understand?

A French officer enters unobserved, carrying his sheathed sabre in his hand.

LIEUTENANT (unabashed). IF I don't capture him, General. Remember the if.

NAPOLEON. If! If!! Ass: there is no such man.

THE OFFICER (suddenly stepping between them and speaking in the unmistakable voice of the Strange Lady). Lieutenant: I am your prisoner. (She offers him her sabre. They are amazed. Napoleon gazes at her for a moment thunderstruck; then seizes her by the wrist and drags her roughly to him, looking closely and fiercely at her to satisfy himself as to her identity; for it now begins to darken rapidly into night, the red glow over the vineyard giving way to clear starlight.)

NAPOLEON. Pah! (He flings her hand away with an exclamation of disgust, and turns his back on her with his hand in his breast and his brow lowering.)

LIEUTENANT (triumphantly, taking the sabre). No such man: eh, General? (To the Lady.) I say: where's my horse?

LADY. Safe at Borghetto, waiting for you, Lieutenant.

NAPOLEON (turning on them). Where are the despatches?

LADY. You would never guess. They are in the most unlikely place in the world. Did you meet my sister here, any of you?

LIEUTENANT. Yes. Very nice woman. She's wonderfully like you; but of course she's better looking.

LADY (mysteriously). Well, do you know that she is a witch?

GIUSEPPE (running down to them in terror, crossing himself). Oh, no, no, no. It is not safe to jest about such things. I cannot have it in my house, excellency.

LIEUTENANT. Yes, drop it. You're my prisoner, you know. Of course I don't believe in any such rubbish; but still it's not a proper subject for joking.

LADY. But this is very serious. My sister has bewitched the General. (Giuseppe and the Lieutenant recoil from Napoleon.) General: open your coat: you will find the despatches in the breast of it. (She puts her hand quickly on his breast.) Yes: there they are: I can feel them. Eh? (She looks up into his face half coaxingly, half mockingly.) Will you allow me, General? (She takes a button as if to unbutton his coat, and pauses for permission.)

NAPOLEON (inscrutably). If you dare.

LADY. Thank you. (She opens his coat and takes out the despatches.) There! (To Giuseppe, showing him the despatches.) See!

GIUSEPPE (flying to the outer door). No, in heaven's name! They're bewitched.

LADY (turning to the Lieutenant). Here, Lieutenant: YOU'RE not afraid of them.

LIEUTENANT (retreating). Keep off. (Seizing the hilt of the sabre.) Keep off, I tell you.

LADY (to Napoleon). They belong to you, General. Take them.

GIUSEPPE. Don't touch them, excellency. Have nothing to do with them.

LIEUTENANT. Be careful, General: be careful.

GIUSEPPE. Burn them. And burn the witch, too.

LADY (to Napoleon). Shall I burn them?

NAPOLEON (thoughtfully). Yes, burn them. Giuseppe: go and fetch a light.

GIUSEPPE (trembling and stammering). Do you mean go alone—in the dark—with a witch in the house?

NAPOLEON. Psha! You're a poltroon. (To the Lieutenant.) Oblige me by going, Lieutenant.

LIEUTENANT (remonstrating). Oh, I say, General! No, look here, you know: nobody can say I'm a coward after Lodi. But to ask me to go into the dark by myself without a candle after such an awful conversation is a little too much. How would you like to do it yourself?

NAPOLEON (irritably). You refuse to obey my order?

LIEUTENANT (resolutely). Yes, I do. It's not reasonable. But I'll tell you what I'll do. If Giuseppe goes, I'll go with him and protect him.

NAPOLEON (to Giuseppe). There! will that satisfy you? Be off, both of you.

GIUSEPPE (humbly, his lips trembling). W—willingly, your excellency. (He goes reluctantly towards the inner door.) Heaven protect me! (To the lieutenant.) After you, Lieutenant.

LIEUTENANT. You'd better go first: I don't know the way.

GIUSEPPE. You can't miss it. Besides (imploringly, laying his hand on his sleeve), I am only a poor innkeeper; and you are a man of family.

LIEUTENANT. There's something in that. Here: you needn't be in such a fright. Take my arm. (Giuseppe does so.) That's the way.(They go out, arm in arm. It is now starry night. The lady throws the packet on the table and seats herself at her ease on the couch enjoying the sensation of freedom from petticoats.)

LADY. Well, General: I've beaten you.

NAPOLEON (walking about). You have been guilty of indelicacy—of unwomanliness. Do you consider that costume a proper one to wear?

LADY. It seems to me much the same as yours.

NAPOLEON. Psha! I blush for you.

LADY (naively). Yes: soldiers blush so easily! (He growls and turns away. She looks mischievously at him, balancing the despatches in her hand.) Wouldn't you like to read these before they're burnt, General? You must be dying with curiosity. Take a peep. (She throws the packet on the table, and turns her face away from it.) I won't look.

NAPOLEON. I have no curiosity whatever, madame. But since you are evidently burning to read them, I give you leave to do so.

LADY. Oh, I've read them already.

NAPOLEON (starting). What!

LADY. I read them the first thing after I rode away on that poor lieutenant's horse. So you see I know what's in them; and you don't.

NAPOLEON. Excuse me: I read them there in the vineyard ten minutes ago.

LADY. Oh! (Jumping up.) Oh, General I've not beaten you. I do admire you so. (He laughs and pats her cheek.) This time really and truly without shamming, I do you homage (kissing his hand).

NAPOLEON (quickly withdrawing it). Brr! Don't do that. No more witchcraft.

LADY. I want to say something to you—only you would misunderstand it.

NAPOLEON. Need that stop you?

LADY. Well, it is this. I adore a man who is not afraid to be mean and selfish.

NAPOLEON (indignantly). I am neither mean nor selfish.

LADY. Oh, you don't appreciate yourself. Besides, I don't really mean meanness and selfishness.

NAPOLEON. Thank you. I thought perhaps you did.

LADY. Well, of course I do. But what I mean is a certain strong simplicity about you.

NAPOLEON. That's better.

LADY. You didn't want to read the letters; but you were curious about what was in them. So you went into the garden and read them when no one was looking, and then came back and pretended you hadn't. That's the meanest thing I ever knew any man do; but it exactly fulfilled your purpose; and so you weren't a bit afraid or ashamed to do it.

NAPOLEON (abruptly). Where did you pick up all these vulgar scruples—this (with contemptuous emphasis) conscience of yours? I took you for a lady—an aristocrat. Was your grandfather a shopkeeper, pray?

LADY. No: he was an Englishman.

NAPOLEON. That accounts for it. The English are a nation of shopkeepers. Now I understand why you've beaten me.

LADY. Oh, I haven't beaten you. And I'm not English.

NAPOLEON. Yes, you are—English to the backbone. Listen to me: I will explain the English to you.

LADY (eagerly). Do. (With a lively air of anticipating an intellectual treat, she sits down on the couch and composes herself to listen to him. Secure of his audience, he at once nerves himself for a performance. He considers a little before he begins; so as to fix her attention by a moment of suspense. His style is at first modelled on Talma's in Corneille's "Cinna;" but it is somewhat lost in the darkness, and Talma presently gives way to Napoleon, the voice coming through the gloom with startling intensity.)

NAPOLEON. There are three sorts of people in the world, the low people, the middle people, and the high people. The low people and the high people are alike in one thing: they have no scruples, no morality. The low are beneath morality, the high above it. I am not afraid of either of them: for the low are unscrupulous without knowledge, so that they make an idol of me; whilst the high are unscrupulous without purpose, so that they go down before my will. Look you: I shall go over all the mobs and all the courts of Europe as a plough goes over a field. It is the middle people who are dangerous: they have both knowledge and purpose. But they, too, have their weak point. They are full of scruples—chained hand and foot by their morality and respectability.

LADY. Then you will beat the English; for all shopkeepers are middle people.

NAPOLEON. No, because the English are a race apart. No Englishman is too low to have scruples: no Englishman is high enough to be free from their tyranny. But every Englishman is born with a certain miraculous power that makes him master of the world. When he wants a thing, he never tells himself that he wants it. He waits patiently until there comes into his mind, no one knows how, a burning conviction that it is his moral and religious duty to conquer those who have got the thing he wants. Then he becomes irresistible. Like the aristocrat, he does what pleases him and grabs what he wants: like the shopkeeper, he pursues his purpose with the industry and steadfastness that come from strong religious conviction and deep sense of moral responsibility. He is never at a loss for an effective moral attitude. As the great champion of freedom and national independence, he conquers and annexes half the world, and calls it Colonization. When he wants a new market for his adulterated Manchester goods, he sends a missionary to teach the natives the gospel of peace. The natives kill the missionary: he flies to arms in defence of Christianity; fights for it; conquers for it; and takes the market as a reward from heaven. In defence of his island shores, he puts a chaplain on board his ship; nails a flag with a cross on it to his top-gallant mast; and sails to the ends of the earth, sinking, burning and destroying all who dispute the empire of the seas with him. He boasts that a slave is free the moment his foot touches British soil; and he sells the children of his poor at six years of age to work under the lash in his factories for sixteen hours a day. He makes two revolutions, and then declares war on our one in the name of law and order. There is nothing so bad or so good that you will not find Englishmen doing it; but you will never find an Englishman in the wrong. He does everything on principle. He fights you on patriotic principles; he robs you on business principles; he enslaves you on imperial principles; he bullies you on manly principles; he supports his king on loyal principles, and cuts off his king's head on republican principles. His watchword is always duty; and he never forgets that the nation which lets its duty get on the opposite side to its interest is lost. He—

LADY. W-w-w-w-wh! Do stop a moment. I want to know how you make me out to be English at this rate.

NAPOLEON (dropping his rhetorical style). It's plain enough. You wanted some letters that belonged to me. You have spent the morning in stealing them—yes, stealing them, by highway robbery. And you have spent the afternoon in putting me in the wrong about them—in assuming that it was I who wanted to steal YOUR letters—in explaining that it all came about through my meanness and selfishness, and your goodness, your devotion, your self-sacrifice. That's English.

LADY. Nonsense. I am sure I am not a bit English. The English are a very stupid people.

NAPOLEON. Yes, too stupid sometimes to know when they're beaten. But I grant that your brains are not English. You see, though your grandfather was an Englishman, your grandmother was—what? A Frenchwoman?

LADY. Oh, no. An Irishwoman.

NAPOLEON (quickly). Irish! (Thoughtfully.) Yes: I forgot the Irish. An English army led by an Irish general: that might be a match for a French army led by an Italian general. (He pauses, and adds, half jestingly, half moodily) At all events, YOU have beaten me; and what beats a man first will beat him last. (He goes meditatively into the moonlit vineyard and looks up. She steals out after him. She ventures to rest her hand on his shoulder, overcome by the beauty of the night and emboldened by its obscurity.)

LADY (softly). What are you looking at?

NAPOLEON (pointing up). My star.

LADY. You believe in that?

NAPOLEON. I do. (They look at it for a moment, she leaning a little on his shoulder.)

LADY. Do you know that the English say that a man's star is not complete without a woman's garter?

NAPOLEON (scandalized—abruptly shaking her off and coming back into the room). Pah! The hypocrites! If the French said that, how they would hold up their hands in pious horror! (He goes to the inner door and holds it open, shouting) Hallo! Giuseppe. Where's that light, man. (He comes between the table and the sideboard, and moves the chair to the table, beside his own.) We have still to burn the letter. (He takes up the packet. Giuseppe comes back, pale and still trembling, carrying a branched candlestick with a couple of candles alight, in one hand, and a broad snuffers tray in the other.)

GIUSEPPE (piteously, as he places the light on the table). Excellency: what were you looking up at just now—out there? (He points across his shoulder to the vineyard, but is afraid to look round.)

NAPOLEON (unfolding the packet). What is that to you?

GIUSEPPE (stammering). Because the witch is gone—vanished; and no one saw her go out.

LADY (coming behind him from the vineyard). We were watching her riding up to the moon on your broomstick, Giuseppe. You will never see her again.

GIUSEPPE. Gesu Maria! (He crosses himself and hurries out.)

NAPOLEON (throwing down the letters in a heap on the table). Now. (He sits down at the table in the chair which he has just placed.)

LADY. Yes; but you know you have THE letter in your pocket. (He smiles; takes a letter from his pocket; and tosses it on the top of the heap. She holds it up and looks at him, saying) About Caesar's wife.

NAPOLEON. Caesar's wife is above suspicion. Burn it.

LADY (taking up the snuffers and holding the letter to the candle flame with it). I wonder would Caesar's wife be above suspicion if she saw us here together!

NAPOLEON (echoing her, with his elbows on the table and his cheeks on his hands, looking at the letter). I wonder! (The Strange Lady puts the letter down alight on the snuffers tray, and sits down beside Napoleon, in the same attitude, elbows on table, cheeks on hands, watching it burn. When it is burnt, they simultaneously turn their eyes and look at one another. The curtain steals down and hides them.)

CPSIA information can be obtained
at www.ICGtesting.com
Printed in the USA
LVOW04s1331010216
473167LV00024B/831/P